The Gallant Cloakmaker: Selected Tales

Elek Benedek

– 150th Anniversary Edition –

The Gallant Cloakmaker: Selected Tales

Elek Benedek

– 150th Anniversary Edition –

Pécs, Hungary
2009

Published by Publikon Publishers/IDResearch Ltd.

Translation © Andrew C. Rouse, 2009

Illustration and cover: Zolta Árvay

Design and Layout: Publikon Publishers/IDResearch Ltd.

Printed by: Molnár Printing House, Pécs

ISBN: 978-963-88505-7-7

2009 © IDResearch Ltd.
www.idresearch.hu

Elek Benedek

"Benedek Elek was born on September 30, 1859, in Kisbacon. He was a writer, journalist and editor and the founder of Hungarian children's literature. He began his studies at the college in Székelyudvarhely and completed them at Budapest University… He died on August 17, 1929, pen in hand." (From the 1972 edition, published in Hungarian in Bucharest by the Ion Kreangă Publishing House.)

2009 sees the 150th anniversary of the birth and the 80th anniversary of the death of the prolific writer Elek Benedek. Practically all of the plots will be familiar to anyone who has read European (or any other) folktales. Here are Puss in Boots and Jack with his beanstalk as well as many other favourite heroes and villains. But these stories have been moulded into an environment unequivocally Hungarian – a Hungary of a century and much longer ago. They are also the products of a master story-teller, and though they may be written down, everywhere the reader feels them come to life with the improvisitive twists and turns of the oral tradition. Even the author's name sounds as though it has been created to be one of his characters, like Lord Otromfotrom.

It has been sheer pleasure to translate this selection from the many tales of Elek Benedek. My thanks go out to Dr. Márta Farkas, who allowed me to borrow the volume from the family villa at the Balaton in order to do so and give me an alibi for antisocial behaviour as I locked myself away.

Martonfa, 20th August, 2009.

CONTENTS

The Tree that Reached the Sky

Once upon a time in a land there never was, across the Briny Ocean, seventy-seven lands away or maybe even further, but anyhow somewhere or other, there lived an aged king. His white beard swept the ground, and if he took one step he tripped two, so old was this king. Yet whatever difficulties age brings, still he loved life, and only one thing better than that: his only daughter, who was so beautiful that you could stare at the sun but not at her. This lovely princess had so many suitors that they knocked one other off their feet, and there were two kings for each finger. The old king would have liked his daughter to find a partner… and then again he wouldn't: for if he thought of his daughter being carried off across the Briny Ocean, never to be seen by him again, his heart hardened and he said to every suitor, "My daughter is young. It can wait."

Even the princess thought that there was time and more before she need take a husband. Each morning she walked out to her garden, and secretly shed bitter tears as she thought that one day she would have to leave behind her the lovely flowers she had planted with her own hand. Who else would tend so lovingly such a delightful garden, full of such beautiful flowers and… yes, of a tree that reached the sky, a tree not to be found in the whole wide world, though her garden had one.

As these thoughts went through the mind of the wonderfully pretty princess, suddenly a whirlwind descended upon the garden, plucking it up into the air so that not a trace was left. When the wind had subsided the princess was sought everywhere, but in vain. The poor old king would have thrown himself into the Danube in his sorrow, had he not tripped upon his beard.

What should they do? Where could they go? Surely the earth had swallowed her up! Yes, the earth. The wind had made it gape open and she had fallen in.

Time passed, and there was no sign of the princess. One night the king saw in a dream that his daughter had been thrust up by the whirlwind into the tree that reached the sky, indeed, into the castle of the nine-headed dragon, who kept her captive and intended to wed his only daughter. You can well believe it, for each leaf of the tree was big enough to hold a country with all its extras included. Now wouldn't it have been good to know which leaf his dear girl was on? Not even his prophets could tell him that.

There was nothing to do but decree throughout the seventy-seven lands that whoever brought back his daughter would receive her hand in marriage and straightway half his kingdom, the other half upon his death.

The decree worked wonders. Princes, dukes and barons came in floods. Each attempted to climb the tree that reached the sky, yet none succeeded: all had to return down before they were halfway up.

The old king was downcast with sorrow. For days he spoke to no-one, and all thought that this woe would be the death of him. But one day a little swineherd came from the king's court and, using the proper formula, said, "Lord and King, I offer you my life and death. Give me leave to climb the tree that reaches the sky. Let my head be stuck on a stake if I do not return with the beautiful princess!"

Great as was the king's sorrow, the palace walls shook as he laughed out loud at the lad's impudence. Two princes were standing by and to be sure they did not laugh, for they were struck with amazement. What did a ragged little swineherd hope for when they, noble princes, had tried their luck in vain? The royal fool was sitting next to the king and grinned from ear to ear. The aged king sought his council.

"What do you think, fool?"

"I think, royal king, that you should throw me out and make this lad your court fool."

"A mad wind blows through a mad hole!" cried out the swineherd lad, now angry. "I'll just show you and bring back the princess!"

"Very well," said the king. "Go, but if you fail to bring back my daughter, just hope that you fall out of a tree and break your neck, because if you don't, then I'll have my executioner break it for you!"

All that the swineherd wanted besides was for the king to have the buffalo with the broken horn butchered and seven pairs of moccasins made out of his hide, as well as seven suits, and to give him provisions for seven weeks.

It must meanwhile be said that the swineherd hadn't set out for the tree that reached the sky like a madman. Among his swine there was a dirty little piglet that none of the other herds paid any heed to, and he alone cared for. When this piglet had seen that not a single mother's son could bring down the king's daughter, he called out to the swineherd:

"You have been kind to me; now listen to what I have to say, for I want to serve you. Did you know that so far no-one has been able to climb the tree that reaches the sky? And if they did succeed, what would they gain from it? That tree has so many leaves that it would take a whole lifetime just to walk a thousandth of them, and how could you know which one the princess was on? You try too. Have the buffalo with the broken horn butchered, have seven moccasins made out of its hide, and seven suits besides, and keep climbing until the last pair of moccasins and the last suit falls from you in shreds. At that point you will reach an outstretching branch. Go right along to the end and step upon the furthest leaf. On that leaf there is a country – the rest is up to you."

The swineherd didn't have to be told twice. He went up to the king, and once the king had given his consent there was no more reason to stay, and he began to climb the tree that reached the sky. He took his little axe with him, and where there was no branch he cut steps out of the trunk and thus progressed ever upward. He went by day and by night, and he had already tied on his seventh pair of moccasins when he reached the point where he was closer to the sky than to the ground. He had clambered up in the seventh pair of moccasins for seven whole weeks, when he saw that they had split apart. There he was, by the outstretched branch of which the piglet had spoken. He set out along it. At first things went easily, because it was good and thick, but then it became thinner and thinner. It was beginning to bend under him, and he wondered whether it might not be better to turn back. But that was out of the question! He closed his eyes and said, "Farewell, world!" took a running jump and leapt onto the leaf.

And, well, what did he see when he opened his eyes again? He'd arrived in a true-to-life country! A country just like the one down on the ground, with towns and villages, woods and meadows, water and everything.

Now the swineherd set off, and walked and walked until he reached a castle that span on a diamond leg and had seven thousand windows, just as it had seven thousand staircases. He would have liked to enter the castle, but whenever he stepped upon a staircase it turned over before him. Some thousand stairs turned before him, and try as he might, he always fell back down them.

You can believe that the swineherd was truly angry. He was going to enter that castle if it took him his entire life! He took out his little axe and just as the wooden staircase was turning in front of him, he swung his axe into it, held on fast to the handle and so swung onto the staircase. Now he could easily walk up the stairs, of which there were exactly one thousand. And as he walked in through the gateway, what was the first thing he should see? Why, the princess!

The princess clapped her hands in startled astonishment and cried out, "How did you get to this place, Johnnie, which not even the birds visit?"

"If you please, I climbed," answered Johnnie. "Now come along with me, your highness, and I'll take you home."

"Oh, do not speak the word, for if the nine-headed dragon with whom I live were to hear it, our lives would be at an end!"

Hardly had the words left her lips when the dragon arrived and caught sight of Johnnie.

"Well who and what is this?" it asked.

"This is my little servant boy," answered the princess. "He couldn't bear to stay below and came up to serve me."

The dragon agreed to let Johnnie stay, and gave him no further tasks but to tend to the poor horse in the stable. But if it should ask for anything he should do the opposite, or it would cost him his life.

Johnnie went out to the stable and looked at the horse, which was such a bag of bones it could not rise from the stable floor. Straightaway he brought it hay and oats, but the horse did not even cast a glance at them. Then he made it a mess of pottage, but the nag did not eat from that either. Johnnie's heart went out to the poor creature, and was lost for an idea to cheer it, but all at once the animal spoke:

"Do not wonder that in my poor condition I turn my head at such fine victuals: I am accustomed to food of another flavour. But my master will not give it to me, for only I know the secret of how to destroy him. And so that I cannot, he wants to starve me to death. Yet I see that you have a good heart. Do what I ask and you will not regret it."

"What shall I do?" asked Johnnie.

"When on Sunday the princess bids you to church do not go, but light the great stack of wood in the courtyard. Leave the rest to me."

Now the dragon had commanded Johnnie to do the opposite of what the horse desired, but even so he obeyed the horse. On Sunday, when the princess called him, he did not follow her to church but stayed at home and lit the stack of wood in the courtyard. In half an hour the stack was no more than a pile of embers. The horse had a shovel of embers taken across to him, and wonder of wonders ate those burning straw embers down to the last ash! At that his power so returned that he could stand, whereupon he made his way to the great pile of embers. Then Johnnie saw that the horse had five legs. In a trice the horse had eaten all the embers from skin and bone the animal became as fat as a barrel.

Once the horse had returned to its original state of health, it said to Johnnie, "Now, dear master, go into the cellar. There you will find a bridle, a saddle and a sword. Bring them up and then let's go hunting. But don't tell anyone why you need them."

So Johnnie went down to the cellar and took up the gear, but as he was coming up the dragon called out at him.

"Where are you off to with that gear, you gnome of a man? You'll die for that!"

"Oh, do not kill me, dear master!" begged Johnnie.

"All right, first draw a pitcher of wine from the barrel and we'll drink that for your sins."

Johnnie drew a pitcher of wine and they drank it up.

"Now that was something!" said the dragon. "Let's drink another pitcher for your father's sins and another for your mother's. We can't have you going thirsty into the next world!"

When they had drunk the two pitchers of wine, the dragon said, "Now give me the sword!"

"Don't kill me, dearest master," implored Johnnie anew. "At least wait until tomorrow, and then we'll fight fair and square. At the moment I'm as drunk as sandy soil!"

The dragon gave him until the next day, then threw himself upon his back and fell asleep, but Johnnie ran with the gear to the horse.

He saddled the five-legged horse, mounted it and off they set to the forest. As they went Johnnie told the horse of his encounter with the dragon.

"Don't you worry about that," the horse consoled him, "because by the time you come to fight we'll have already killed the dragon. Just attend to me. In this forest lives a wild boar; inside its head there is a rabbit, in the rabbit's head a matchbox and inside the box seven hornets. If we destroy the hornets it will be the end of the dragon, too, for in them lies his strength."

Hardly had they reached the forest when the wild boar came rushing at them, brandishing its fearful tusks. Johnnie was petrified this really was the end of them, but the horse kicked out sideways at the boar with its fifth leg so powerfully that it fell to the ground. At this Johnnie took courage and slashed the boar's head in two with the sword. As soon as the two halves fell apart, out leapt the rabbit. At once the five-legged horse set off in hot pursuit and soon overtook it and gave it such a kick with its fifth leg that it fell unconscious. Now Johnnie split the rabbit's head in two, and sure enough, there inside was a matchbox with the hornets buzzing around inside it like some village meeting.

"Just you wait, you soon won't be buzzing like that!" said Johnnie, and putting the matchbox on a flat stone he smashed another flat stone upon it so that the hornets were turned as flat as pancakes.

By the time they arrived back the dragon was at death's door and begged Johnnie not to kill him but to take all the gold, diamonds and precious jewels in the castle. Johnnie spared the dragon's life and set off to gather up all the treasure. But as he left he heard the dragon grumble, "Take it all, take it. I'll get it back, together with your soul."

"All right, we'll see about that," thought Johnnie to himself, but first he gathered up all the treasure and then returned and cut off all nine of the dragon's heads.

"Now take your own soul!" said Johnnie.

Oh, but wasn't the princess joyful when she learnt of all that had happened, and in her happiness she said to Johnnie, "Now Johnnie, you are mine and I am yours whether here above or down below!"

So overjoyed was Johnnie that his heart almost burst out of his body, but then he suddenly became saddened. Because although he'd be very happy with the princess right where he was, even so it was better down below. And what would happen when autumn came and the leaf upon which they were perched fell from the tree? Every bone in their bodies would be smashed to smithereens. He'd managed his way up all right, but it wouldn't be so easy to get back down again.

The five-legged horse noticed that his master was unhappy and straightway found out which way the wind was blowing.

"I know why you're so sad, little master, but just leave things to me, there's more to me than meets the eye. Pack together everything you need. Sit on my back, but close your eyes and do not open them until I give the word."

They bestrode the horse, and once they had closed their eyes the horse said, "Now open your eyes!"

They opened their eyes again and could you believe it they were in the old king's court. In a trice Johnnie dismounted, lifted the princess off the horse and quickly whisked himself back onto the horse so that no-one would see such a ragged lad beside the princess and galloped away like the wind. But he remained in the town and from all his treasure bought expensive clothes and built a palace, and one day sought an audience with the old king.

Of course nobody recognised him in his shining, golden raiment. Not even the princess, except with great difficulty. But then joy flooded her to the depths of her heart, for her head had been heavy with sorrow at the idea that never in her life would she see her deliverer again. The old king kept his word: to Johnnie he gave half of his kingdom together with his daughter, and they had such a wedding feast that every lady had a prince for her dancing partner. For seven days and seven nights they banqueted, eating and drinking and dancing. On the seventh night the old king kicked his leg in the air and dropped dead, so Johnnie inherited the entire kingdom.

And if you don't believe me, go check it out for yourself.

Lovely Cerceruska

Once upon a time, in a land far, far way, across the briny blue, there lived beside the bust-in side of an old oven an old widower and his two beautiful daughters. And these daughters were so beautiful that they might have been princesses. (I'm telling this true just as I saw them!)

Well, right next-door there lived a widow-woman. And she called across one day to the older daughter, Cerceruska, saying, "D'you hear me, Cerceruska? Tell your father he ought to marry me, and then I'll bathe you in milk and butter!"

Cerceruska was overjoyed and went to tell her father what the widow-woman had said.

The old man didn't wait for a second offer and married the neighbouring woman straight off!

Now wasn't there a happy life for one week and two! But that's just how long the fun lasted, for in the third week the poor girls got beaten more than they were fed. But they weren't going to put up with that, oh no! they'd rather go out into the wide, wide world. They agreed to go berrying in the woods and never to return. When they had prepared themselves and were outside the gate, the wicked old hag called after them:

"Whatever water you drink out of the print of an animal, that animal you will become!"

Well, the younger daughter did not hear the curse, but Cerceruska did, and when they arrived in the wood, she made her sister promise that however thirsty they should become, never to drink from the print of a beast. But while they were berrying, the two sisters moved apart and the younger couldn't assuage her thirst with berries. She knelt down at the print of a doe, drank from it and was immediately transformed.

Cerceruska sought her sister everywhere. She called out but received no answer. Then she began to weep bitterly, so bitterly that the woods rang with her sobbing. Shaking through her tears, she espied a little deer. The animal bayed at her as she ran towards her. And how she licked and fawned at her. To be sure, this was her little sister.

Cerceruska cried even more bitterly, then hugged the doe and led her across the woods. As they were wandering through the trees, Cerceruska espied a hunter approaching them with his hound.

Now she was really frightened! What would happen to them if the hunter caught sight of them? Surely he would shoot her sister? Frantically she looked around to find a hiding place for the two of them. Then her eyes fell upon a hayrick, and they crawled into it. Hardly had they hidden when the hound comes sniffing at the base of the rick and poking its nose into the hole. Then, suddenly turning, it bounded back to its master, leaping up at the hunter and whining as if with hunger. Digging into his bag, the hunter drew out a piece of bread and threw it to the hound.

Quick as a flash, the hound took off with the bread as though it had been whipped. It galloped across to the rick, pushed the bread in through the hay to Cerceruska and raced back to its master, whining loudly. Again the hunter gave the hound bread, and once more the hound bounded away with it. A third time it quickly returned, and a third time begged for bread.

"Just a moment!" said the hunter, "I'll give you bread the third time too, but this time I'm going to see where you're taking it, for I don't believe you've eaten it yourself!"

But you can imagine that his eyes nearly popped out of his head when he saw a beautiful young maiden and a young doe poking their heads out of the hayrick.

Poor Cerceruska was horribly afraid that this would be the end of herself and her sister. Surely now the hunter would shoot them down?

The hunter called out to her, "Hey, who and what are you? How come you here, beautiful maiden?"

To which Cerceruska answered, "I'll tell you, Hunter, if you promise that no harm shall come to my doe."

"Just come out, the both of you, and don't fear, I won't hurt you."

At this, Cerceruska crawled out of the rick, her sister with her. She told the hunter who and what she was, and who and what the little doe.

Hearing the tale, the hunter said, "Don't cry and don't be downhearted, you beautiful maiden. For I am the King of White Russia, and I'll take you to my court to wait on my wife the Queen. Your sister will have a fine life. I'll keep her in a garden of her own where she will come to no harm.

And so they made their way to the king's palace. Cerceruska became a handmaiden of the Queen, and the doe was kept close in a garden of golden trees in which golden birds sang by day and by night.

Meanwhile let it be said the King of White Russia had hardly been married a single year. But his wife was not the daughter of the Black King for nothing: she was as threatening black as a thunderstorm. Bringing such a beautiful young girl as Cerceruska to be her handmaiden was all that was needed! One day, in a mood foul and black she stood before her husband and scolded, "Get rid of that wench, d'you hear? She's nothing but a good-for-nothing idle hussy!"

But the King replied," Hold your tongue, woman, and let her be! Why should she work?"

Time passed. One day the King went hunting with his entire court, leaving only the Queen and Cerceruska. This was all that the evil-hearted Queen required. Using sweet, honeyed words, she beckoned the girl into the garden where the little doe was kept. This garden had a bottomless lake. When they reached the edge, the Queen said, "Look into it, Cerceruska. Look into it and see how beautiful you are."

Cerceruska leant over the water to look in, and at that moment the Queen suddenly thrust her in. Seeing this, the little doe began to keen bitterly, but the Queen only said, "Keen on, keen on all you like, just don't speak."

When the King arrived home he asked where Cerceruska was.

The Queen mumbled and grumbled that she didn't know, perhaps court life wasn't good enough for her and she had run off.

The King was utterly despondent and had everyone search for Cerceruska high and low throughout his kingdom, but to no avail. One day the Queen became very ill. She demanded from the King that he should cut out the heart and liver of the little doe, for a wise old man had told her that she would only be cured after having eaten the heart and liver of the doe.

The King told her that this was all dreams and midsummer madness, but the Queen was insistent and wouldn't leave him in peace. And so the King thought to himself, "I'll go hunting, shoot a deer, and bring back its heart and liver to be cooked. After all, a deer's a deer, they've all got the same shape of heart and liver.

But while the King was out, the Queen – who was as healthy as you or I – arose, and called for a butcher. Out they went to the garden to kill the doe. The sad little animal saw the Queen and the butcher with his sharp knife. She knew immediately that they were there to take her life. In vain did they attempt to draw her now here, now there, she dashed blindly around the garden out of their reach.

Meanwhile the King came home, and went straightway to the garden, where the doe happened to be standing at the edge of the bottomless lake crying out

> Step out, dearest Cerceruska
> From the lake's depths, that's my wish,
> From the belly of the great fish.
> They're sharpening the knife for my soft hide,
> They're bringing the bowl for my red blood!

Hearing this, the King called out to his entire court to dredge the lake. The fish was caught and cut open, and out stepped Cerceruska.

Wonder of wonders! Cerceruska was alive, and one hundred times more beautiful than before. The little doe leapt over her head with joy and was immediately transformed back into a maiden. But the Queen was so puffed up with the poison of her anger that she exploded!

Without more ado, the King commanded that the evil-natured woman be cast into the depths of the bottomless lake, and the very same day he wed fair Cerceruska. The celebrations lasted seven times seven days, after which the young couple rolled away in a walnut shell.

Let them be your guests tomorrow!

Gácsęra[1]

Once upon a time, if ever, let's just say it was a good while ago, I had a hen. And believe it or not, it was the size of an eagle. Not that I profited at all from its prodigious size, for no matter how hard I spied on it and waited, not one egg did it lay. I thought to myself, I won't keep it a moment longer, I'll take it to market and sell it. And that's what I did, and as soon as I set it up for sale the world and his wife gathered round, staring like a heifer at a new gate. And then, suddenly, would you believe it, in front of all that throng, my hen laid an egg the size of a pumpkin. Of course, now everyone wanted to buy it, promising bagfuls of gold, but she wasn't for sale now, oh no! I grabbed my hen and took her home again, thinking "She'll lay still more for me at home, and then I might get a hundredfold more gold."

So I took her home, and waited. And waited. Waited for my hen to lay again. But all in vain: days and weeks passed, but not one more egg did the hen lay. "Well, if that's the case," I thought to myself, "I'll get her to brood. Perhaps if I sit her on an egg she'll become a better layer." And so I sat her on an egg, and there she sat, night and day and day and night, brooding for all she was worth, but would that egg hatch? Not so much as a crack. And if I went up close, to take a peek at the egg, my hen whacked me in the eyes with her wings. "I'll have to wait till she gets off the egg to visit the dung heap," I thought to myself. And that's what I did. No sooner was the hen off the egg, than I rushed up to it and picked it up. And would you believe it, it was cold as ice. So I held up to the sun to see if it was clear, thinking I might at least have a good fried egg out of it. But it was as dark as a deadlight. What on earth could be in it?

---

[1] Roughly pronounced "Garchera".

So I broke it open, and out fell a ream of paper, all nicely folded and covered in lovely handwriting. And what was written was the tale I'll tell you now.

Once upon a time, far away across the briny sea and a flea's jump and a sparrow's hop, and even further, where the curly-coated, bald-eared Mangalica Boar roots, right there lived a poor man. And in the country where the poor man lived it was so unbearably hot that everyone lived under the ground. Even the king. Everyone was poor there, and you were a lord or a duke if you had four bees or twelve walnut trees. For every man woman and child of that land lived off honey and walnuts. And the man of whom I speak had only one bee and a little walnut bush. And this one little bee gave him all his honey. You can imagine how the bee was cared for, like an only child. It even had a name: Gácsera.

But one day, this Gácsera simply took off and flew up, up from the underground and disappeared as if it had been swallowed up.

My but the poor man was sad, as was his son. They sought high and low, above and below ground for Gácsera, asking everyone they met if they had seen their bee. But nobody had. Days and weeks passed, and of Gácsera there was no sign. The poor man said to his son, "Be off with you, son, and find Gácsera, or we'll both die of hunger. And if you find him, ask him to come home. We'll feed him poultry and cinnamon cakes, bathe him in milk and butter and rub him down with logs of wood.

And so the son set off, wandering through seven times seven countries. For seven nights and seven days he went his way, through forest, field and flood. Here he went and there, asking everywhere, "Have you seen Gácsera?"

"What's that when it's at home?" they asked. "Is it man or beast?"

"To be sure an animal, yet more than a man, for so far it's kept myself and my father alive."

"What kind of animal is that?"

"To be sure, a bee," replied the lad.

And how they laughed at the poor lad.

"You silly dumpling, how do you think you'll ever find a bee?"

Never mind. The lad went on his way, and as he was crossing a meadow, what should he see but Gácsera, harnessed to a plough next to a gigantic, longhorn ox. Behind them went the ploughman with his whip, flicking it at the ox and at poor Gácsera too.

"Move, you brutes."

Poor Gácsera's neck bowed at the yoke, and the lad was close to tears to see the sad lot of his hapless bee.

Over he went to the man at plough, greeting him with due respect.

"Excuse me, but at which market did you buy the one of your oxen?"

"Which one?"

"The one without horns but with wings."

"Oh, I didn't buy that one at any kind of market." said the poor man. It came up to me the other day and begged to be put to use, saying I wouldn't regret it.

"Dear Sir," says the poor lad, "that bee was ours, and if you don't find it in your heart to return it, we'll die of hunger for sure."

The ploughman had a soft heart, and said, "Well, if you put it like that, then I'll hand it over. Go with God's blessing."

At once he released Gácsera from the yoke, and the lad made his way homeward with him. But Gácsera complained all the way that his neck hurt and his legs hurt and he hurt all over. The poor lad racked his brains over how to put Gácsera to rights.

As they made their mournful way they came to a mulberry tree. The lad tore off a fistful of mulberry leaves and began to rub Gácsera's neck with them. Well, God bless you, what do you think happened? No sooner had he rubbed Gácsera's neck with the mulberry leaves than a mulberry tree grew out of Gácsera's neck, where it grew bigger and broader and higher until the highest branch hit the sky and the others spread as far as from here to the back of beyond.

The lad was overjoyed, and why not indeed? From now on they would not only have honey but mulberries to eat, as many as they wished!

And in this mood he made his way home and called out to his father through the crack:

"Come on out, father! I've fetched home Gácsera, and just look what else I've brought."

But his father couldn't come out, for while his son was away he'd become so fat with starvation and sorrow he couldn't fit through the crack. He could just about poke his noddle through, to see what his son had brought. And instead of being happy, he gave the poor lad a good scolding, and if he'd been able to squeeze through the crack the boy would have got a beating for good measure for bringing home a mulberry tree when he couldn't even get through the crack!

So that was that: the poor man stayed underground and his son above ground, with Gácsera and the mulberry tree. And you should have seen what a crop of mulberries it gave! A veritable sea! All kinds of people came from far and wide to look. A thousand sat upon a single branch, eating the mulberries. But however hard they tried, nobody could reach the topmost branch, though they wanted to enough, for however many mulberries were on the lower branches, eventually they all got eaten. The whole lot! You see, there were more poor people there than mulberries.

How on earth were they to pick the mulberries from the top branch? They couldn't climb up it, and so they went far and wide in search of all the sticks in the land used for beating fruit from the trees, and threw them up into the top of the tree. But all to no avail. The sticks caught up and stuck up in the branches, but not one berry fell down. And when they ran out of sticks, they started tossing up good, hard clods of earth. Those got stuck up in the tree too.

Suddenly guess what happened? What happened was that it began to rain. The hard clods of earth up on the top of the tree began to soften, and a meadow full of flowers grew around them with grass more lush than human eye had ever seen.

The poor lad was sad to see this grass growing so lush, for he would have liked to mow it down, but where was he to find a scythe? It took but a moment's thought, and without further ado he made his way to the wood to catch himself two hundred rabbits, for as you know, rabbits are notoriously good at mowing with their tails. He went straight to King Hare, made a good bargain with him and the king promptly ordered two hundred rabbits before him. Off they went with the poor lad to mow the meadow down.

The rabbits climbed up to the top of the tree, but by the time they reached the top the slenderest blade of grass was thicker than my arm. The poor rabbits laboured hard enough, I can tell you! And in that thick grass all their tails fell off. Ever since, rabbits have been as small as they are today, with such tiny scuts instead of proper tails.

If the rabbits' tails had been much stronger, then my tale would have been much longer.

Rabbitherd

Once upon a time, and what a long time go it was, seven times seven generations ago, there lived a poor old widow and her three sons. They were as poor as church mice. They cooked water and thickened it with sticks, and that's how they lived day in, day out. At last the lads had enough of this bitter life, and decided to leave home and go they knew not where, just so as not to have to live this way another day.

One day the oldest said to his mother, "Mother, cook me a scone in the cinders, for I'm off to seek my fortune."

This the poor woman did, and her boy set off to see the world. He went over hill and dale, through lands of every kind, until he came upon a golden well: Settling down beside it he took out his cinder-baked scone, but just as he began to eat, out runs a little mouse and says, "Hear me, you poor boy. Give me a crumb of your scone. I haven't eaten that much in seven days."

"I couldn't care if you haven't eaten in seventy-seven days," answered the lad. It's not even enough for me."

The mouse squeaked sadly and disappeared into a hole. The lad set off again until finally he arrived at the royal city. He made his way straight to the royal palace, sat at the palace gate and waited to see what fortune would befall him. What do you know, but that the king himself came out. He sees the lad and greets him, asking,

"What can I do for you, my fine fellow?"

To which the lad replied, "Your majesty, in whose hands are my life and death, I am seeking service, if only I could find some."

The King then said, "Come inside, my boy. My courtyard contains a hundred rabbits; I'll place them in your care. Drive them out to the meadow, but be warned! If you lose but one, you'll lose your head as well."

The next morning the boy drove the hundred rabbits out to the meadow, but sure enough, as soon as they reached it the one hundred rabbits ran off in one hundred directions. The boy quivered with fear! Not even daring to look in the direction of the palace, he took to his feet and ran, not stopping until he reached his home.

There, he related his sad chance, where he had been and everything that had befallen him, at which the second son stood up and announced that he would try his luck and, as God was his witness, he would look over those hundred rabbits to his last breath.

But his journey into the wide world went the way of his eldest brother. He too sat at the golden well to eat, and denied the mouse the crumb it asked for. Then he went on his way until he reached the royal city. He entered the service of the King, but on the very first morning as he drove the rabbits out to the meadow, the hundred rabbits went their hundred ways.

Sadly and with a heavy tread the lad returned home, where now the youngest brother decided to venture forth and try his fortune. His mother cooked him a scone in the embers of the fire, as big as a cartwheel, and thus armed he went out into the wide, wild world, until he reached the golden well. Just as was settling himself down to eat, out pops the mouse, who pleaded to him in the name of God for just one crumb, as it had not eaten for a whole fortnight.

"Gladly, little mouse," replied the youth. "I'm hoping I won't have to live off this scone for overlong."

The mouse thanked him, saying, "Now, you poor boy, good deeds are rewarded with goodness. I asked your brothers for the same, but as they would not help me, neither did I assist either of them.."

At that the mouse ran into its hole, bringing out a tiny horn.

"This horn I give to you," said the mouse. "Put it away until there comes a time of need."

"But what use can I make of it?" asked the youth.

"Just take it," said the mouse, "and in whatever danger you may be, blow upon it and all will turn for the better."

"Well," thought the boy to himself, "If it does no good, still it can do no harm. I'll take it with me."

Thrusting the horn into his bag, he went on his way, not stopping until he reached the royal city and the King's palace gate, where he made himself comfortable.

At last the King arrived, and asked, "What brings you here, poor fellow?"

The youth told the King the truth; that he was looking for a good place where he could enter service.

"In that case, you've come to the right place," said the King. "I have a hundred rabbits in need of a canny rabbit-herd, for as yet I've found none to my liking.

At this they shook hands, at the same time the King warning him that if he lost but one of his rabbits he would lose his head into the bargain.

So that was that. The next morning, the youth drove the rabbits out to the meadow, but they did not so much as sniff the grass but scampered off in a hundred directions.

"Hi, there, where are you off to?" cried the lad.

Then he remembered the horn. He drew it out, blew upon it, and the hundred rabbits turned and flocked together like so many sheep.

The King saw all this from the top of the palace balcony, and shook his head. He could in no way imagine what devilish craft the lad had used over his rabbits.

"Now just a minute," he thought to himself, "we'll make sure that at least one of those rabbits goes missing out of the hundred. If no other way, I'll put him to the test."

At that, he commanded a serving girl to go down to the meadow with a sack and ask the rabbitherd for a rabbit in the King's name. The girl went down and asked for a rabbit, but the youth told her that he wouldn't give a rabbit even for the King, his head was worth more than that.

"Say what you like. There will be guests at the palace, and the King will have your head and mine besides if there's no rabbit on the table," said the girl.

And while they were bickering, what should appear from nowhere but the little mouse, which called out to the boy, "Just give him one. Don't be afraid, and trust the rest to me."

Heeding the mouse's words, the boy grabbed a rabbit by the ears, thrust it into the bag and sent it off with the girl. But at that moment the mouse scrambled into the sack, and before the girl had gone ten paces had gnawed through the bottom. Out jumped the rabbit and returned to its fellows as though nothing had happened. Meanwhile the mouse took a great cowpat and put that in the sack, which the girl carried homeward as if nothing had happened.

Evening arrived. The youth was driving the one hundred rabbits in through the great gate, when the King came up to him, cursing so that all the court trembled.

"Come here, you hangman's fodder! What did you send me in that sack?"

To which the boy replied, "Let me be blinded if it wasn't a rabbit, my lord."

Then they called for the serving girl.

"What did the rabbitherd give you, girl?"

"Your majesty, as sure as my life is in your hands, he really did give me a rabbit."

"Ho!" said the King. "Well, I've never eaten such a thing in all my born days. And so where is this rabbit?"

They counted the rabbits once, twice and thrice, but always there were just one hundred.

"Now hear me, you poor lad," said the King, "I have never had a herder who could drive the rabbits without losing one. What do you desire?"

"Just a sack of money, your majesty, for we are very poor at home."

At that, the King had a goodly sack filled with money, so big that the youth needed twelve oxen to carry it home. Were they rich? They were so rich that they are still alive today, if they have not died.

Strong John

Once upon a time and a long time ago, over the waves and far away, seventy-seven lands and a crooked mile from here, there lived a poor woman and her great useless lump of a son. The poor old women wove her hands to the bone from morning to night, her arms and legs hardly pausing in the hard, physical work, but for all that her good-for-nothing lazybones of a son lifted not so much as a finger to help her, but lounged around in the dust from dawn to dusk, dribbling the dust from one hand to the other.

Oh, but the old woman was sad, and almost worn to death with the sorrow and bitterness of it all. What would become of her only child when her eyes closed for the last time? The boy was so awkward, such a lazybones, that he wouldn't even lift the Lord's blessing to his mouth.

But one day John spoke up, and asked his mother, "Mother, what are those men hammering at so mightily?"

"My dear son, those men are building a house, and that is what they are hammering."

In a flash, John leapt up so energetically that his mother's eyes and mouth remained fixed wide open with amazement, and said, "I'll go over there too, mother. Maybe I can be of some use."

When he reached the builders they were struggling with a fifty-foot rafter, but they had neither the spirit nor divine strength in them to raise it. John clapped his hands together in astonishment and said, "Can't you even lift that?"

"Away with you, you good-for-nothing ash-grinder," shouted one fellow, "or I'll stick your neck under a tree!"

"You'll do what? Not so fast! It's a shame to feed you a half-portion – no, a whole! – if you can't even lift that twig!" Out of the way!"

And with that he grabbed the rafter and raised it as though it was no more than a stick.

You can believe the sudden respect John gained. He was the first to be called for wherever there was building to be done. He handed up the heaviest of wood and earned so much money he didn't know what to do with it.

And how happy his mother was! To have such an upright son, who'd support her to her dying day! She went off to the priest to boast of how he was this and that… The priest was a miserly man. He'd never had a servant, but now he thought he might just take on John for a pittance. He'd just bought a large area of overgrown scrubland – the powerful lad could clear it for him.

He told the woman his intention. How pleased the poor dear was! She ran home and led John straight back to the priest. The agreement was speedily concluded. It was this: the priest would supply John and his mother with food, drink and clothes, and when the work was over John would receive a new pair of moccasin thongs. These would be cut out of the back of the priest or of John, depending upon which was angry with the other.

John arrived at the priest's home to begin his service on New Year's Day. The next morning he was given a little cold corn porridge and told to herd the flock onto the scrubland which he was meanwhile to clear, and not to come home till evening. Yet his food pouch was as flat as if it had been struck by lightning.

This didn't worry John. He herded the sheep, left them to graze and then gathered up the dry branches and lit such a massive fire that the flames licked the heavens. Once the embers were glowing he took two lambs, skinned them and spitted them on a good hard cherry skewer, roasted them until they were beautifully crunchy and feasted himself so well that a king would have exchanged places with him.

In the evening he went back home with the flock. When he arrived the priest asked him how big an area he had stripped away.

"All of it, saving your presence," answered John.

"All? All of what?"

"Why, of those two spotted lambs, saving your presence. Maybe the reverend is angry with me?"

Angry? No, no, not at all. You did the right thing. Do the same again if my wife doesn't put anything in your pouch."

The priest scolded his wife roundly for causing such damage through her stinginess, even though it had been he who had ordered nothing to be placed in the pouch, but there was no-one else upon whom he could vent his anger.

And so it went all winter. When spring came, the priest went to see how John was doing with the clearing work.

Not one bush had been cleared away, and there was John, sleeping like a baby among the ewes. The priest woke him up and began to scold him, but all John did was to ask, "Are you angry with me, Your reverence?"

"No, no, of course not, you scallywag! Just give me your back so I can cut out the moccasin thongs, because you didn't keep to our agreement!"

"First let the reverend keep to his part, which you haven't! You haven't given my mother a scrap to eat, and myself but little enough!"

"There's no argument to that," thought the priest. He had nothing but trouble until the scrubland was cleared. The next day John was surprised to see that his pouch was full, with a white loaf, bacon, curd and even a bottle of pálinka.

"Well," he thought, "now we can start clearing the land."

He started work with an axe, but it went slowly. "I'm not going to get anywhere like this," he thought. He cast away the axe, grabbed the nearest bush with his two bare hands and started tearing the scrub up like the women do the hemp.

In two days he had torn out everything: trees, bushes, shrubs, even pepper-grass; then he rolled into a pile as high as a church and set it alight.

What a magnificent fire! It was so great that at sunset it didn't get dark. It was seen from the village and the people took fright that the entire world was on fire!

They sounded the alarm with the church bell; some took up axes, others buckets, and all ran to the fire as though their lives depended upon it. Only when they got there they discovered that it was only the priest's scrubland and not the world that was on fire.

John roared with laughter and the people went, disgruntled, back to their homes. In the morning the priest asked John, "Is there much more to clear, John?"

To which John answered, "Not a straw, your reverence!"

"So what did you do, where did you clear it to?"

"I burnt it down to the last twig. Didn't you see the great fire in the night?"

"Of course I saw it, but they told me it was the next village on fire."

"Perhaps you are angry with me, your reverence?"

"No, no, not at all…" although really the priest was so angry he nearly exploded.

Neither the priest nor his wife had any idea of what to do with this gallows-bird of a John. Night and day they racked their brains over how to rid themselves of him. At last the priest came up with a plan. He called John over to him, and said, "Here is food and clean linen. Take it off to the forest for your brother Nicholas, who's been tending the swine there for this past year and is probably in rags, poor thing. When you find him, herd the pigs home together.

John set out for the great forest in search of the herd of swine that had never existed. Because any clever person could have seen in advance that the only reason the priest had sent him into the forest was to be devoured by some wild creature.

John went on and on through the wilderness. He visited every place that the priest had explained he might find Brother Nicholas, but found neither him nor any other living being.

He had been hunting for a week and was considering whether or not to return home to ask further about the possible whereabouts of Brother Nick. As he was deep in thought he heard a rustling, crunching and munching such as it made by a herd of swine.

And so it was. A great herd of swine was making its noisy way through the undergrowth, followed by a great black figure, evidently the swineherd.

John was very happy to have found the priest's pigs after all. He shouted out at the top of his voice, "Hey, Brother Nick, wait a moment! I've brought bread and clean clothes, everything!"

But Brother Nick merely went on his way, grumbling as he went. He was a bear, not a man – I can see him as though it were yesterday!

He was after the wild pigs in hope of catching one for his supper. John was extremely angry that Nicholas had not so much as turned his ear. He ran across to him and slapped him hard in the ribs.

"Good day to you, Brother Nick! Won't you stop for a word with a poor man? The Reverend has sent fresh clothes: put them on, now: your old ones are worn to rags!"

The bear was startled and suddenly ran up a tree and growled at John from up there.

"Stop fooling: come down from that tree and put on your smock!"

But the bear remained motionless and growling.

"Nrrr…nrrr…nrrr…"

"Don't you "no" me, you blighter!" shouted John. "Come down, and Now, Brother Nicholas!"

Well, he could speak all he wanted to the beast. John was getting more and more angry, and in the end he grabbed the tree and pulled it up by its roots so that it was felled to the ground along with Brother Nicholas.

Brother Nicholas groaned piteously and in his pain he roared so that the forest shook.

"Didn't I tell you not to fool with me? Have you hurt yourself? Well then, put on that smock!"

Now Brother Nicholas wasn't fooling. He raised himself up on his hind legs and gave John a cuff that made him see green and red.

But now John's patience was at an end.

"Nrrr…nrrr…" Uncle Nick kept growling.

"Now you just put that smock on or I'll make you dance!" shouted John.

Well he could speak or shout, use pretty or harsh words for all he liked, it was like talking to a wall. Brother Nick just growled and kept cuffing John, left-right-left-right.

"So that's how it is! Right!"

He grabbed smock and pants, grabbed hold of Brother Nick and dressed him nicely, moreover giving a good buffeting to the limbs that didn't bend as they ought. When he was done with the dressing, he grasped Brother Nick by the arm and took him to help drive the pigs homeward. But he could crack the whip at them for all he was worth; not one went the way he wanted, and if he actually hit one of them it would turn and snarl at him, brandishing its tusks. Seeing that he was getting nowhere he cut out a twenty-foot beech branch and began to apply it from the side. This worked, except that a fearsome wild boar turned and rushed at him.

"Stop right there, pig!" said John, "I'll soon teach you some manners," and at that he smote it such a blow on the head that it died in an instant. Then he left it in Brother Nick's care while he herded up the others.

Ah, but Brother Nick cared for it so thoroughly that he had eaten it to the last morsel by the time John returned.

"You could at least have left one half, but I don't mind, just help me drive the rest home."

But the bear just growled: "Nrrr…nrrr…nrrrr…"

"What do you mean by no, damn you! Now! This instant!" shouted John, and gave the bear such a blow that it set off immediately.

The next evening they arrived home without further incident.

When the priest saw the sea of pigs he went clammy cold with fear. John drove the swine into the barn, cooked one for Brother Nick's supper and then went in to the priest and said, "Now, your reverence, I've driven your pigs home for you, but not for the world would I keep such a swineherd as Brother Nicholas. I swore at him in vain: he wouldn't put on clean clothes, even though he wasn't wearing a stitch because the old ones had fallen from him. He didn't want soft shoes or even cooked meat. He eats it raw, and a whole pig at a time at that! Not for the world did he want to come home. If I were you, your reverence, I wouldn't keep him a moment longer."

"I won't, no indeed, son. Just chase him out to the edge of the village," prompted the priest in his hurry to free himself of the bear.

Out went John, grabbed the bear by the ears, took him out to the fields and said, "There's one way up and another down, Brother Nick. Go wherever your eyes lead you."

And that's exactly what the bear did: it ran straight for the forest as though its life depended upon it.

"Now," thought the priest, "at least I've got rid of that, but what in the world shall I do with all these wild pigs?"

He called in John, and said to him, "John, my boy, I see those pigs are good and fat. Kill them for me at dawn tomorrow."

John rose with the sun, killed the swine one by one and then began to singe them. By morning he'd singed away all the priest's straw.

The priest told him to go to the magistrate and ask for a bundle of straw.

John went to the magistrate, who told him, "Go to the garden, my boy, and you'll find a large haystack. Take as much as you can carry."

So John went down to the garden, lifted one end of the haystack, placed himself under it, and lifted the entire stack. But he couldn't fit under the hayloft, so he lowered the stack, tipped the loft over a little, lifted the stack again and when he reached the door called out, "Many thanks, your worship!"

"Hey!" cried out the magistrate, "wait one moment, you ruffian, don't you take all my straw!"

But John cared not one whit, and took the whole lot to singe off the priest's pigs' bristles.

Now the priest could free himself of the pigs, but not of John.

Again he hatched a plan to destroy him. In his yard there was a deep, dry well, covered with a millstone so heavy that a dozen men could not move it. The priest said to John, "Remove that stone and place the meat and the bacon into the well so that it doesn't rot."

Of course John was able to move the stone. He went down into the well to pile up the meat, which took twenty-four men to hand down to him. For a while they just handed down the meat, but then the priest had the millstone put back over the well. John waited and waited for the meat to start being handed down again, but when he saw that he was waiting in vain he started back up to see what was happening up above.

When he reached the top his head struck something heavy. He looked and saw that the millstone had been replaced.

"All right, then," thought John. "This hat has rather a large brim, but you greet a person according to the hat he wears."

He placed his head in the hole in the middle of the millstone, raised himself into the yard and wished the priest a very good morning. He said, "Thank you for the hat, your reverence, but the sun has done no harm to me as yet and I don't wear headgear like that."

The priest was eaten with rage and vexation. Worry gnawed at him that he could not rid himself of that thorn in the side John. As he fretted the order came that either he should enlist in the king's army or send someone in his place to fight against the French. The priest was beside himself with joy: now he really would free himself of John. He gave him a great white horse, four weeks' provisions, even money: two bright coins.

Only when John was mounted upon his steed did he ask the priest, "What must I do when I get there, your reverence?"

"Nothing, my boy, except fight."

"Well if it's just fighting, God bless you, your reverence. Thanks for your kindness."

John went off to war and arrived just as the fighting was hottest between the two armies. John dismounted from his horse and hobbled it, then made a fire for himself, took out his food pouch, placed a cauldron of water over the fire and once it was boiling poured in the grains for a corn porridge. Just as the porridge was bubbling merrily the enemy started firing at his campfire and a massive cannonball landed fell right next to John.

"Hey, don't you fire over here!" shouted John, "there are people over here!"

Well, the enemy heeded John but little, and cannonballs and gunshot rained around him in showers. Again John called out.

"I told you not to throw things; if you hit me or ruin my porridge it will go hard with you!"

Hardly had the words left his mouth when a cannonball took away his porridge, campfire and all as though they had never been. But now the joke was wearing thin with John. He leapt up from where he lay, grasped a young birch by the roots and ran brandishing it to the enemy. There he buffeted and rained blows down upon the enemy so that some ran and others were killed, but not one man jack remained.

Then he went off again, lit another fire, and made such a corn porridge that its steam wafted up to the heavens.

Just as he was getting into his porridge, up came the king. He thanked him graciously for having saved the country from its enemy. He made him a duke and gave one of his daughters to be his wife.

When the priest heard this he nearly jumped out of his skin with joy for having rid himself of John after all. John's mother was overjoyed as well that the Lord had seen fit to so elevate her son.

John lived happily with his wife, and is still living, if they haven't died yet.

The Valiant Tailor Lad

Once upon a time that never was and seven times seven lands away there lived a king. And this king had two gardens in which grew silken grass and nothing else. One day the king decided to mow down his grass so that his horses could eat silken hay. He brought together an army of men with scythes and ordered them to go into his garden and mow down his grass.

The bravest of the mowers stepped forward and said to the king, "Beg pardon Your Majesty, you can stick our heads on spikes, but we won't mow down your silky grass, 'cause there's three giants a-living in the one garden and three bears in t'other, and not even Your Majesty's army could handle them, let alone us. We'd be dead as dodos before our scythes so much as stroked the grass."

Just at that moment a journeyman tailor lad wandered into the court. Hearing what the mowers were saying, he immediately offered his services to the King.

"Your Majesty, just leave it to me; I'll get rid of those giants for you, and the bears too."

"Listen here," said the King, "You don't look much of a hero to me. But if you prove to be the man you say you are, then I'll give you half my kingdom."

At that they slapped hands in agreement, the tailor lad only asking the king for a rabbit, a lump of curd and a bladder full of blood.

Well that wasn't much of a request. In a flash he was brought a rabbit from the game park, some curd from the corral and a big boar's bladder bulging with blood. Off went the tailor lad to the back garden, the one with the giants in, where the giants happened to be strutting along with their hands trailing behind them in the soft, silky grass. Up goes the tailor lad, doffs his hat and greets the giants, who reply by showing their sharp teeth and saying, " What are you doing here, you wisp of a human?"

"Looking at the grass, to see if it's ready for mowing."

"I'll give you mowing," said the oldest giant. "Just you wait and see!"

"Oh, no, your Largeship, you just wait a minute!" answered the tailor lad. "We'll soon discover who knows most."

The giants set off a-guffawing, but they laughed so uncontrollably that the underworld echoed to the heaving of their bellies. Once they had caught their breath, the youngest giant said, "Come along then, let's have a running race."

"Don't mind if I do," replied the tailor lad. "You start."

And so the youngest giant began to run. But the moment he was off the tailor lad released the rabbit, and cried out to the giant:

"Call that running! Why, my younger brother can run faster than you!"

And sure enough, the rabbit passed the giant in the flash of an eyelash as if he wasn't even there. The giant didn't even try to compete with the little tailor.

Then the middle giant stood forward. He took an immense rock in his hand, crushed it into tiny pieces and devoured it to the last grain.

"Follow that if you will, you little shrimp!" he said to the tailor lad.

"Oh, that's nothing!" replied the cocky tailor.

He put the curd on the rock and began to squeeze it, saying, "Look, I can even squeeze water out of a stone!"

"Ho, that boy really is strong," said the oldest giant to the other two. "Best if we stay on good terms with him."

They gave up competing with him but pressed him to stay the night in their home. He ate a hearty supper and then they prepared for bed. But the tailor lad was suspicious, thinking that if he fell asleep the giants would destroy him. And so he slipped a sheaf of straw among the sheets in his stead, with a bloody bladder on the pillow for a head, and then slid under the bed to take his rest.

Sure enough, at around midnight along came the oldest giant with a sword, and smites the bladder such a blow that the blood splashed up between his eyes. At that he went off to his companions and joyfully showed them the bloody sword: all their worries were over; he'd killed the tailor lad. The giants returned to their beds immediately and promptly fell asleep. This is exactly what the tailor lad was waiting for. He slit their throats, spiked their heads on a sword and in this way took them next morning to the King.

"Well, my lad," greeted the King, "you surely are a valiant fellow. "Now just rid me of those three bears and half the kingdom will be yours. Do you need anything?"

"Not really, Your Majesty, just a barrel of wine. Order it to be taken out to the bear garden and I'll take care of the rest."

The barrel was taken out into the garden, and as the carriers departed the tailor boy stave in the lid, and then lay in wait behind a tree for the bears. It wasn't long before they shambled up and set to work at the barrel. They didn't stop till they had sipped up every last drop of wine, but the wine so affected them that they lost the use of their legs and fell motionless to the ground. At once, the tailor lad walked across, sliced off the bears' heads with the giants' sword,

skewered them through its sharp point and in this way took them triumphantly to the King.

"Your majesty, I have also killed the bears."

The King was dumbfounded. What was he to do? Give half of his kingdom to this rapscallion of a tailor? He dearly regretted his promise and cudgelled his brains over how to get rid of the youth. After much thought he said to the tailor lad, "Now, boy, you've earned half of my kingdom, but I'm not going to give it to you until you've brought my mother-in-law back from Hell."

"Don't you worry, Your Majesty, I'll bring her back for you. Just get me a large buffalo-cart and have a large cask of water placed upon it."

You can imagine the King gave him the cart with a good heart. He'd have given him a hundred instead of one, just so as he'd go to Hell, for he hoped that if the demons didn't rip him to pieces, then his mother-in-law would destroy him with her eternal, infernal tongue.

Off went the tailor lad and arrived at the gates of Hell. There he set a-swishing and a-cracking of his whip. In the trice the Devil himself arrived in a rave and a rant and asked:

"Hey, boy, what's all that din you're making? What are doing here at all?"

"I've come for the King's mother-in-law to take her home."

"Not a chance!" spluttered the Devil.

"It's best you know that I have here a cask of holy water. If you don't give her to me I'll bless this place and build a chapel here."

Oh but the Devil was in a flummox! He ran into Hell and told old Pluto what the lad wanted. Well that set Pluto a trembling too, in fact all the devils were affrighted and without further ado they expelled the King's mother-in-law from Hell. They put her straight on the cart so that the lad would take her away.

And so it was that the valiant tailor lad took home the King's mother-in-law. The King had been feeling very jolly at the thought of the tailor perishing in Hell and not having to share his kingdom. But all his jollity disappeared when he espied his mother-in-law. In fact he was so scared that he didn't even wait for her to arrive at the palace; he ran hither and thither like one whose eyes had been pulled out and didn't stop until he reached the end of the world.

The people waited for the King to return, but in vain: a week passed and longer, and the King did not come back. Then they got tired of waiting. The entire population of the country gathered in the royal city and pronounced the tailor lad their new king.

That's how it was. Now it's over. That's the story. Go find out for yourselves if you don't believe me.

The Golden Tulip

Once, in a far-off country, beyond seven times seven lands and across the silver sea, there lived a King, and this king had a son. When the prince grew into a youth, he said to his father, "Father, I must leave, and I shall not return until I have found myself the most beautiful girl in the world. She will be my wife."

"Right, my boy," answered the king, "Go, with God's blessing, and may good fortune accompany you."

And so the prince set off, over hill and dale, until he reached a vast forest. Making his way through the forest he came upon a fish splashing around in a puddle.

The fish called out to him, saying to the prince, "Free me from this puddle, good youth, and place me in the river, for I shall die here".

The prince took the fish out of the puddle and took it to the river. Here the fish said, "Take one of my scales, and if ever you are in trouble, just drop it in the river water and I shall appear in an instant to help you."

The prince took one of the fish's scales, threw the fish into the water and went upon his way until he came upon a black raven that hat entangled itself in the branches of a tree. No matter how hard it flapped its wings and scrabbled with its legs, it could not free itself.

The raven cried down woefully to the prince.

"Free me, good youth. Trust me, you won't regret it."

The prince climbed up the tree and freed the raven, which pulled out one of its feathers with its beak and gave it to the prince, saying,

"Good deeds are returned with good, young lad. Should you ever be in great peril, just shake this feather, and I will be by your side."

The prince bade farewell to the raven and carried on his journey, until he noticed a grey old man standing by a spring. He would have liked to bend down to drink, but was so stiff in the joints that he could not bend an inch. He called out to the prince, "Be a good lad and help me. I'm dying from thirst, and I can't bend down to drink."

The prince took off his helmet, filled it to the brim with water and gave it to the old man to drink from.

"Now, young man," said the greybeard, "you have done me a great service. Here, take two strands of my hair, and should you ever be in danger, just let them fly in the wind. They'll find me sure enough, and I'll go to the ends of the earth to aid you."

The prince put away the two strands of hair, bade the old man farewell and went upon his way. It was not long before he came to the edge of the forest and beyond that to a great city. His eyes stared and his mouth gaped in wonder, for the whole city was dressed in mourning.

Going along the street, he met a dwarf of a man with a beard that reached the ground. He asked him, "Tell me, uncle, why and for whom is the city in mourning, that everyone is dressed in black?"

"I'll tell you, young one," said the little man, "and we've got good reason, too. The king has a daughter, so beautiful that none in the world can compare. And this girl's got it in her head that she'll only marry a man, no matter who he be, who can hide so she can't find him. That person can try three times. If he fails twice, then that's no great matter. But fail a third time, and his head will be stuck on a stake. So far ninety-nine have tried their luck, and there are ninety-nine heads on stakes. Why don't you try too, young man, so your head can be the one-hundredth?"

To that the prince answered, "Well, there will be a hundredth head or there will not, but if that girl is as beautiful as you say, I'll try my luck."

At that very moment a girl of wondrous beauty came that way in a carriage drawn by six horses. The prince had never seen such beauty; when he looked at her his eyes were dazzled."

The prince asked the little dwarf, "Who is that girl?"

"She's the princess," replied the little man.

The prince needed no more. He went straight to the royal palace and went before the king.

"Your Majesty, I have heard that ninety-nine lads have tried their fortune and failed. I have but one life and one death, and I too will do my best."

"My boy," replied the king, "I am sorry from my heart, for you seem to be a handsome, upright lad. But all is in vain, for I must please my daughter. I have no other child. So try your luck and hide so she'll not discover you."

Meanwhile the princess arrived home. She entered the chamber and said to the young prince, "Better if you do not try your luck, prince. Be off with you, or your head will join all the others."

"What do I care?" said the prince. "What will be will be. Without you my life is not worth a pipesworth of tobacco."

The prince left the palace and sadly roamed the length of the city, then out to the meadow and from the meadow to the forest. All the way he was thinking of where he could hide that the princess would not find him. Suddenly he thought of the fish: maybe it could help him?"

He made his way to the river bank and took out the scale. Sure enough, up swam the fish and asked, "What's your trouble, oh Prince?"

The prince told the fish his troubles.

"Oh, don't worry your head about that," said the fish. I'll call the largest fish here in a trice and have him swallow you. You can be sure the princess won't find you for as long as the world turns and two days more!"

Sure enough, the little fish twisted and turned, and immediately a massive fish came after him. It opened its mouth, which was as big as a house, and in jumped the prince, who ambled down to its stomach, where he walked about as if he was in a palace.

Meanwhile the princess set off with the court behind her. The princess sought out the prince everywhere, and after half a day of searching came to the riverbank. She ordered the largest fish to be caught, because the prince was in its stomach. The royal fishermen were called to the river and they caught the great fish and opened up its stomach, whereupon the prince stepped out.

Well, the prince hadn't done too well in the first test. But he tried again. He went sadly on his way, and as he entered the great forest the raven came to mind. He shook the feather, at which the raven flew up to him, at once asking, "What is your trouble, dear master?"

The prince told him what great trouble he was in. At this, the raven began to croak, and at once ravens came flying from every direction. The forest was black with them. They asked all together, "What care? What care?"

"Do you know a good hiding-place?" asked the prince's raven.

They flew up in a cloud across the forest. The prince rushed after them until he came to a mountain so high that its peak scraped the sky. Inside the peak was a deep crater, into which the ravens placed the prince.

But to no avail. The princess found him there, too.

The poor prince was crestfallen. Now his head would end up on a spike like the rest. But, he thought to himself, he had but one life and one death: he might as well try a third time. He took out the two strands of hair which the old man had given him, and released them in the wind. Hardly had he done so when the old man came and asked him, "What are your troubles, my son?"

"Don't even ask me, worshipful uncle! I'm supposed to hide somewhere that nobody will find me, or else my head will end up on a spike."

"If that's all, well I can help you easily. Who do you want to hide from?"

"From the princess, worshipful uncle."

"Well then, I'll show you," said the old man, "how I can lead you before her eyes and she still won't see you."

At that he grabbed the prince's neck and twisted it so the prince turned into a golden tulip. Then he stuck the tulip in his hat and went into the royal city.

At that moment the princess approached in the opposite direction; she was just setting out in search of the prince. She spied the gleaming golden tulip, and in her nicest voice begged the old man to give it to her.

"Oh, what a lovely tulip. Do give it to me!"

"That I will not," said the old man.

"I'll give you so much gold that you'll become lord over every nation."

"I won't give it," said the old man. "Not for all the most wonderful treasures in the world!"

In vain did the princess implore; the old man wouldn't give her the tulip. There was nothing to be done: the princess went sadly on her way in search of the prince. But she didn't find him. On the third day her search came to an end, and then the king announced that the prince could come out of hiding, for he had won the hand of the princess.

The old man heard the proclamation and twisted the tulip once, so that it became once more a prince. The prince went straight up to the palace. A priest was summoned at once and there was a sumptuous feast. After the feast they went to the prince's home where the party truly began in earnest with a hallelujah and a hey-nonny-no!

Perhaps they're still dancing if they haven't died.

Otromfotrom

Once upon a time or maybe never, I know not where but even so somewhere there was a poor man. This poor man had nothing in the whole wide world but a little cockerel.

Once the poor man became so famished that his eyes saw green and blood-red, and he clawed at the wall in his great agony. He wasn't going to suffer any more, thought he to himself, but he'd kill that cockerel and eat it down to the last bone.

"Now, you cock," said he to the duck, "go put some water over the fire so I can cook you."

"Don't kill me, master," clucked the little cockerel. "I'll scratch out a penny for you from the garbage heap, buy an egg with it and feast you as though you'd eaten from the king's table."

To this the poor man replied, "So be it, I don't mind, but there'd better be an egg or it's the knife for you!"

Out ran the little cockerel, but not to the garbage heap: instead he ran out to the forest. There he met a rabbit.

The rabbit asked, "Where are you running, little cockerel?"

"Just over here to the well, my rabbity friend. I've heard that whoever bathes in this well will gain gold."

"Take me with you, little cockerel!"

"With a good heart," answered the cockerel, "just bring along a few friends with you."

Off ran the rabbit, and gathered together another fifty rabbits. The little cockerel led them straight to the king's court, and announced to the king that Lord Otromfotrom paid his respects and that he sent these fifty rabbits as a gift.

The king said to him, "Tell me, little cockerel, is your master such a great lord?"

"To be sure he is," answered the cockerel. "My master is such a great lord that he has a gold watch in each of his pockets!"

The king thanked him for the generous gift and gave the cockerel a gold coin. Now the little cockerel ran like the wind, ran until he had almost panted away his soul. By the time he arrived home, his master was laid out on the floor from the terrible hunger he suffered. The little cockerel straightway produced some eatables from nearby and fed him back to health.

Time passed, and once again the poor man was near starved, and once again determined to kill the cockerel. But now, too, the cockerel promised to bring him back some food and the poor man left him alone.

Once again the cockerel ran into the forest, but this time he met a wild boar. The boar asked him, "Where are you running, little cockerel?"

The cockerel told him about the wondrous well he knew the whereabouts of.

"Then take me with you," said the boar.

"I will indeed, if you bring fifty companions."

And so it was, as he wished, and the wild boars were led in their turn to the king's palace.

The king was appalled. He couldn't for his life imagine where in the world so many wild boar could be brought together. Once again he gave a gold piece and again the little cockerel saved his master from starvation.

Even so, for a third time he had to stir his wits for hardly a week had passed before his master was laid out with hunger again.

On the third occasion he took three deer to the king.

"Tell me," the king asked him, "why does your master send me so many gifts?"

To this the cockerel replied, "To be sure, Your Majesty, as my life and death are in your hands, it's because he wishes to ask the hand of your daughter."

"Is that so, you little cockerel? Well, I'd be happy to give it if he came after her."

The little cockerel ran home and told his master what had happened.

The poor man was petrified!

"Cursed cockerel! How could you put me in such danger? You! The king will have my head for this!"

"Just come with me," said the cockerel, "and fear nothing."

What could the poor man do, but set off? When they arrived at the forest, the cockerel told him, "Wait here, master. I'll go on ahead to the king's court and say that you have been robbed of your golden finery, horses and coach. The king will send everything for you."

Thus it was, just as he said. He ran with great agitation to the king and told him that his master had been robbed of everything by the forest thieves.

To this the king said, "Thank goodness they spared the life of my future son-in-law!"

Immediately he sent for his finest attire, had six golden-maned horses set in the traces of a glass coach, and in this way set off for the poor man. Poor soul, he was shivering naked behind a bush. In a trice he was dressed in the fine, golden attire and taken to the king's court. The king was beside himself with joy that he had would have such an upright, clever son-in-law. They had a magnificent feast where the wine flowed from Hence to Thence and back again.

But all feasts come to an end. Now take home your bride, poor man! His brain boiled with thinking of where to take his delicate princess, when even the hovel in which he lived was not his own. A row of coaches lined the entrance and all the nobility wished to see his palace and the princess's future home.

As he was sitting disconsolately up crept the little cockerel, and said, "I can see you are deep in woe, dear master, but do not be overcome with bitterness. I'll help you in your trouble, you just leave everything to me. I'll run on ahead and everything will sort itself out."

And off he ran, and found along the roadside a herd of cattle. He called over to the cowherd, "Do you hear, man, if anyone asks you who owns this herd, say that it belongs to Lord Otromfotrom, and you won't regret it."

And indeed the wedding guests did ask, and the cowherd said that the bests belonged to Lord Otromfotrom, down to the last heifer's tail.

The king was immensely pleased to discover how wealthy his son-in-law was.

Meanwhile the little cockerel had reached the forest. And in that forest was a golden palace spinning on a cockerel's spur. In this palace lived twelve robbers. In ran the little cockerel and with great agitation told the twelve robbers to hide somewhere in Lord Jesus' name because the king was coming with his entire army in order to impale the lot of them. Oh but weren't the robbers frightened, and every man jack of them hid in the hayloft. Without a moment's hesitation the cockerel set fire to the hay and all twelve robbers were burnt to a cinder. At that he ran out of the palace to receive the guests.

Well, wasn't there singing and dancing then! This time the oceans of good liquor ran from Thence to Hence!

When the feasting came to an end the poor man called the little cockerel to him and said, "Now you little cockerel, never in my wildest dreams did I ever see myself as a great lord in this life. And I can thank you for it all, so tell me, how can I reward you?"

"I don't need anything," said the little cockerel, "I just wish one thing from you, and that is that when I die you will give me a good burial."

And so the poor man promised: why shouldn't he have. Next day in came a servant and announced that the little cockerel had perished.

To which Lord Otromfotrom said, "If he's dead, cast him out!"

And so they did, but the little cockerel had only simulated death. He wasn't dead, oh no, and straightway went up to his master.

"I see you are an ungrateful man," he said.

You can imagine that now Lord Otromfotrom promised him meadows and mountains immeasurable.

The following day the servant brought the news that the little cockerel had really died and this time Lord Otromfotrom changed his tone and commanded a great funeral for the little cockerel, so glad was he that he had really died.

But Lord Otromfotom still lives with his wife, if he has not died since.

Helen, Loveliest in the World

Once there was, or maybe there wasn't, seven times seven lands away and beyond, at one time then there lived a poor man and his daughter. This girl was so beautiful that people came from afar to gaze at her in wonder. And for her beauty she was named Helen, Loveliest in the World.

So much was the name of Loveliest Helen upon the lips of the people that it reached the ear of the king, who happened to be an eligible young man, and from that moment he could find no rest either by night or by day. There was a painter in the court and to him the king said, "Go to this Loveliest Helen and paint her for me so that I can see whether she is as lovely as people say. Because if she is I'll take her for my wife."

Off went the painter, found Loveliest Helen, painted her and took the portrait back to the king.

"Here it is, Your Majesty. She's the spitting image of the painting. In all my born days I have never seen anything so beautiful!"

The king looked at the painting over and over again, his eyes and mouth wide with amazement. Straightaway he called out to his seneschal and ordered him to harness six velvet carriages and bring back Loveliest Helen with all her people.

Well, they could do that easily enough. One carriage would have been enough, too, for apart from her father Loveliest Helen had nobody in the world. They sat Loveliest Helen inside the carriage and her father up next to the driver, and set off for the royal palace. Sometimes they went slowly and sometimes fast, and then they arrived at a deep forest. As they were going through the forest, up popped an old witch with her daughter. Both of them were ugly as sin. The old woman hailed the carriage.

"Stop there, driver. Let me into the carriage and I'll be of service to you."

"Out of the way, old hag," snapped the coachman. "Can't you see this is the king's carriage?"

Loveliest Helen heard all this. She thrust her head out of the window and said, "Never mind, just let her in. I want this to be a good day for everyone."

At that she sat the witch and her daughter opposite her and the coachman drove on. A little later they arrived at a great river. Here the witch suddenly grasped Loveliest Helen, took out her two beautiful eyes and thrust her into the river. The coachman and the poor old man saw none of this and drove on.

When they arrived at the royal palace the king rushed out to help Loveliest Helen down. But he practically turned into stone when he caught sight of the old hag and her daughter!

"This Ugliest of Uglies is no Loveliest Helen!" cried out the king in a tremendous rage.

The poor man looked, as did the coachman. They swore by heaven and earth that they had brought Loveliest Helen with them and that this gross maiden had only got into the coach at the forest. But the old woman also swore by heaven and earth that she was the poor man's wife and that this was their daughter, Loveliest Helen, she'd just got darkened along the way.

"So be it," said the king, "I will not go back on my word. If I wished to marry her in her beauty, I'll marry her in ugliness, but you, you man of poverty, I will cast into a dungeon to the end of your days for neglecting to look after the fairness of your daughter."

For all the old man explained that not once had the hood been raised throughout the journey, that the sun had not shone upon his daughter, that the old witch must have done away with his daughter: the others were more persuasive and the king believed them and had the old man cast into a dungeon.

Meanwhile Loveliest Helen was taken further and further downstream by the current of the river. Then it washed her up onto the bank right in front of a fisherman's hut. An old fisherman and his wife lived in this hut, and these were awoken at around midnight by the most bitter wailing. The fisherman's wife spoke:

"Do you hear, old man, someone's crying at the door?"

"Aye, old woman, I can hear it too," said the old fisherman. "I'll take a look to see what's happening out there."

Out went the old fisherman, and there in front of the door sat a maiden, sodden to the skin and weeping to herself. As he stared he saw that the lass had no eyes, but for all that the tears ran down her cheeks like a spring shower and Wonder of Wonders each teardrop turned into a diamond pearl.

The old fisherman asked her, "Who and what are you, you poor girl?"

Loveliest Helen told him who and what she was and what had befallen her.

"Cheer up, my lass," said the aged fisherman. "Come on in. You can live here to the end of your days. And we have no children of our own."

"The girl thanked him for his kindness and went in, but even so she was unable to still her tears. And as she wept the diamond pearls fell endlessly from her eye-sockets.

At that the old fisherman said, "That will be enough of the weeping! Stop that crying, for I will not rest until I find your eyes again."

He took the mass of diamond pearls and set off with them into the wide world. He sold them from town to town, and you can be certain that every woman and maiden wished to buy them, but the old fisherman said he'd only sell them for two eyes. Oh, but didn't they laugh at him everywhere he went! Old fool! Who would give him their eyes?

And so on he went. On and on, until he arrived at the royal city. Once there, he made his way straight to the ugly queen. He showed her the dazzlingly beautiful pearls.

The ugly queen was so delighted when she saw them that she practically jumped out of her skin. She asked how many sacks of gold she should give for them.

To this the old fisherman answered, "I wouldn't take all the gold you have in your entire country, but only two eyes, Your Majesty."

The old witch came in and her daughter told her what foolishness the old man was asking.

"Well, give her Loveliest Helen's eyes," suggested the old witch. They're no use to you anyhow."

Oh, wasn't there joy! They sought out Loveliest Helen's eyes, gave them to the old man, and laughed heartily at the "old fool" as he left.

The old man set off and did not stop until he arrived home. Loveliest Helen was still weeping, for she did not believe that eyes could be found to replace her own. But find them the old fisherman had indeed. He simply popped them back in place and now Loveliest Helen became a thousand times more lovely than she ever been before.

Time passed. The old fisherman went fishing and took Helen with him. As they were fishing along the riverbank, along came two hunters in a boat who were shooting duck. One of them shouted out to the other, "Look over there! Do you see that girl?"

"I do indeed!" said the other, "but she's so beautiful that I'm going blind from looking."

"God is not God if that's not Loveliest Helen!" said the first.

"Your Majesty speaks the truth. It surely is Loveliest Helen!"

For the two hunters were none other than the king and his seneschal, and immediately they moored up on the riverbank. They ran up to the girl.

The king greeted her and asked, "What is your name, you beautiful maiden?"

"Once they called me Loveliest Helen, but now I do not know if I deserve the name, for I have not looked into a mirror this twelvemonth."

"Well if it's a year that you have not looked into a mirror believe me you are a thousand times more beautiful than before. You'll come with me this instant!"

"Just a moment!" spoke up the old fisherman. "I have some say in that matter!"

"Speak all you like," said the hunter, "for know that I am the king!"

Now Loveliest Helen interrupted.

"The old fisherman is right, Your Majesty, for I can thank him for my eyes."

Then she told him everything that had happened. The king sent the seneschal home for two carriages. In the one he sat with Loveliest Helen, while in the other sat the old fisherman and his wife. He told the seneschal to go home in the boat to make room in the coach.

They soon arrived home and as the carriage turned into the gateway the king cried, "Out of my house, hags!"

He had the old witch and her daughter hauled out of the palace and had both of them quartered and the pieces displayed at the four gates to the city. The poor man was immediately released from the dungeon and such a feast was thrown that news of it spread through seven and seventy lands.

That's how it was, that's the end of the tale.

Daft Stephen

Listen to me, children, and I'll tell you the tale of Daft Stephen.

It was like this. Once there was a poor man who had three sons. All that this poor man had in the world was a bull, and when he died he had nothing else to leave to his sons.

But it would have been better if he had left them nothing at all, for they were also left with the problem of how to divide up the bull. The youngest, who because of his simpleness was known as Daft Stephen, suggested that they kill the bull, sell its meat and share out the proceeds. His two older brothers wouldn't go along with this, if for no other reason than it was the simpleton who had made the suggestion. Yet they didn't know what to do. They didn't even feed the bull, for they were forever bickering: You feed it! I won't! It's yours just as much as it's mine! And in the end the poor bull became so thin you could count his ribs.

Nevertheless, in the end they agreed that each of them would build a stable, and whoever's stable the bull entered would own the entire animal. They set to with a will, and the two older brothers built stables fit even for princes. Meanwhile poor noddle-headed Stephen botched together a mean lean-to of green branches. His brothers laughed their heads off.

"Oh, you poor fool! D'you think the bull's as daft as you are? D'you think he'll so much as look at that shed?"

And that's how things stood. When all three stables were complete, they let the bull into the yard. It was a good, hot, fly-biting day. The bull flicked its tail and started charging around the yard, until, for some reason or other, its careered into Stephen's stable.

That's the truth! The bull now belonged to the fool. His brothers grumbled a great deal, but Stephen said nothing, but merely took up a pouch and led the animal into town to sell. On their way they came to a birch tree. The wind was blowing hard and the birch was creaking loudly. Stephen came to a halt and wondered what the birch was saying. In the end his weak head convinced him that it was asking, "Creak! Rustle! How much for the bull?"

"I'll sell it to you for one hundred forints," said Stephen.

"Branches and leaves, then sell it to me!" said the birch.

Stephen tethered the bull to the trunk of the tree and waited to be given his money. But the birch gave him nothing.

"Let's see the colour of your money, mate!" he cajoled the birch.

But the birch just creaked and groaned and said, "Boles and hollows, I'll give it tomorrow."

"Oh, well," thought the halfwit to himself. I'll get the money tomorrow," and with that he returned home.

Back at home his older brothers asked him, "Now, you idiot, what did you sell the bull for?"

"One hundred forints."

"And who bought it?"

"A birch tree."

His brothers fell about laughing left and right, but the daft lad said nothing. The next day he went to the birch tree, but all he found of his bull was its bones at the end of the tether. The wolves had eaten it in the night.

He asked the birch tree for his money, but the only answer was, "Boles and hollows, I'll give it tomorrow."

"All right, tomorrow then."

And he went home. The next day he returned, but again all the birch tree replied was "Boles and hollows, I'll give it tomorrow."

This went on for three weeks. By this time even the halfwit thought this was going beyond a joke. Taking an axe, he told the birch tree, "Give me he money this instant, or I'll cut you down!"

"Boles and hollows, I'll give it tomorrow."

"Oh, you will, will you? Just you wait and see!"

He grasped the axe and swung it into the trunk so hard that the tree cried out with the pain. And as soon as he wrested out the axe, out too poured a shower of gold. So much gold poured out that it filled his pouch to the brim.

"So it was worth waiting after all. At least I've got some interest!"

And at that he went home, and once he was home he poured out the precious gold into a bucket, covered it with a riddle and put it out under the eaves. His brothers were practically killed by curiosity as to where he had got all that gold; even more so when the mad lad showed no inclination to spend even one piece, continuing to live on porridge just as he always had done.

"Look, the idiot doesn't even know what money's for!" said the oldest to his brother.

They conspired to steal the gold – they'd certainly know what to do with it.

They emptied the bucket clean of gold and replaced it with wheat jam. One day the foolish lad looked into the bucket, and saw that there was no gold in it. Unconfounded, he tied a tablecloth around the top of the bucket and set off to sell the wheat jam.

When he reached the village, he began to cry out, "Come and buy my wheat jam! Buy my wheat jam!"

And the villagers asked him, "What in the world is wheat jam, boy?"

"Ah, it's a remedy," answered Stephen, "which, once tasted, will cure even the half-dead."

My, how the folk gathered together! Everyone wanted to purchase some of the wonder drug, but when they had smelt it, they laughed the daft lad to his face and went off in as many directions as they themselves in number.

"Yeuch! - Yeuch!" they cried out.

"Yeuch, to be sure," the lad called out after them.

By evening he had reached a town, where he asked for accommodation at the grand home of a great noble. He was given a place to lay his head, and put his wheat jam in the barn. But the pigs sensed the smell, burst into the barn and gobbled it up to the last drop.

What a fuss the lad made when in the morning he realised that he had no wheat jam! He announced that he was the king's exchequer, was right at that moment on his way to the king and would lodge a complaint that all his gold had been stolen. At that the noble was very much frightened and gave him so much gold just so that he wouldn't complain to the king that he could hardly carry it off.

Home he went with all this money and his older brothers were dumbstruck with wonder that the halfwit could once again acquire so much money.

They asked him, "How and why have you so much?"

At which the daft lad replied, "For wheat jam."

His brothers needed no more. They too filled buckets with wheat jam and made their way to the next village. They called out "Buy wheat jam! Wheat jam for sale!" until their voices were hoarse.

The whole village ran up, but so hard did they beat the brothers out of the village that they could hardly run off. They tried their luck in another village but fared no better.

Already they loathed their mad brother, but now they were incensed and determined that come what may they would snuff the life out of him. They went to the magistrate and told him that their brother was consorting with the Devil; he was forever piling his house with money and now he wanted to destroy the village. The magistrate believed them and so did the villagers, for what the daft lad was doing was certainly devilish. The village elders decided to shut Daft Stephen in a barrel and throw it over the dam.

And that's what happened. They sealed him up in a barrel, and because it was Sunday they placed the barrel in front of the church, intending to take him off to the water after the service and throw him over the dam.

While the people were in church the mad lad began to cry out, "It's no good your trying to force me! I won't be Lord Lieutenant! I won't be Lord Lieutenant!"

At that very moment a coach and four passed by with a lord form another land inside who heard what was being called out from the barrel. He ordered the horses to a halt and went across to the barrel.

"What are you shouting, man?"

"That I won't be Lord Lieutenant, I'd rather be hanged!"

"Well there's no need to shout," said the noble. "Come on out, we'll change our gear and I'll sit in the barrel. You can have my coach and horses."

And so it happened, just as the strange lord said. Stephen climbed out of the barrel and the noble clambered in. Stephen set off in the coach drawn by the four horses, and when the people came out of church the lord began to cry out at the top of his voice, "I'll be Lord Lieutenant, people! I'll be your Lord Lieutenant!"

"You'll be fish food!" thought the people, but they said nothing, but raised the barrel, took it to the water, and threw it over the dam.

Now everyone thought that that was the end of the satanic Stephen, but as they set off home, their spirits at ease, across the dam came a coach and four with Daft Stephen cracking the rawhide whip at a great rate.

Much was the wonder and consternation.

"Where in the world did you get all that?" the people asked.

"Below the dam!" answered Daft Stephen jauntily. "There's enough down there for six villages. If you don't believe me, come and see with your own eyes!"

The folk tumbled after him in their hurry. Stephen paraded his coach and four along the bank, and the people saw the reflection in the water.

"What do you know, the fool's right!" shouted the people, and quick as a flash toppled over each other into the water. The entire village was swirling around in the water, priest, bellman and all – only the priest's old wife, who had arrived on crutches, didn't jump in. The priest had a great wide hat, and that didn't sink to the bottom but floated on the surface. The old priest's old wife caught sight of it and, stretching out her crutch, beat it harder and harder, saying to her husband, "Go further in, dear sir, and get the best! Go further in!"

Indeed the whole village went so far in that not one person came back.

And so Daft Stephen took possession of the whole village and became a noble the like of which the region had never seen. And if you don't believe me, go and look for yourself!

Peter and Paul

There once lived a poor man. He was called Peter, and he had as many children as holes in a sieve and one more besides, but all his wealth was a single cockerel. His neighbour, Paul, was a wealthy farmer, yet he was always complaining.

One day Paul said to Peter, "Neighbour, your cock spends too much time scratching around in my garden. It's really too much to bear. If I can catch him, I'll wring his neck."

Peter said nothing, but thought long and hard about what to do with the luckless bird.

"It won't be long before I lose it anyway, so I'll give it to his lordship, and maybe get something in return."

At that, he grabbed the cockerel and took it up to the lord.

"Is there a christening or a wedding in the house, Peter, that you're bringing me a cockerel?" asked his lordship.

"Nothing at all, sir. Just you enjoy it, along with your family," replied Peter.

"Well, I don't understand it. Wouldn't it go down well with your own? God knows there are that many of you, Jacob himself would be jealous."

"True, your lordship, very true, but how should I give meat to my children when there's hardly enough bread to go round. Better that they don't taste it."

"Then, you foolish man, sell it and buy bread for your family."

"Ah, but sir, if I go into town, that's two days' walk, and before I return I will have eaten half the price of the cock."

What could his lordship do? He couldn't dissuade Peter, and so he commanded the cook to roast the cockerel for lunch. When lunch was ready, he sat Peter down at the table with the others. That made seven of them. When the cockerel was brought in, his lordship said, "Now, Peter, you must serve the cock, but make sure that everyone gets his rightful portion. Do so, and I will reward you, but if you fail, I'll have you stripped and given twelve lashes."

At that, Peter set the bird before him, cut off its head, and placed it on his lordship's plate, with the following words:

"The head is yours, as you are the head of the family."

Then he cut off the neck, and put it in front of her ladyship, saying, "Neck and head are one, and so the neck is for the lady."

After that he carved off the two wings and gave them to the boys to help them to write, and the legs to the girls to help them to dance.

Now Peter said, "Everyone's had their rightful portion, so I'll eat mine!" and at that polished off the "rest".

The lord and his family fell laughing at Peter's jest, and happily rewarded him richly, giving him bull, cow and calf.

Peter made his way home in good humour. Paul saw his rich reward, and was hotly envious of the fortune the cockerel had brought his neighbour.

"Just you wait, Peter," he thought to himself, "I'll give five cockerels to his lordship, and then I'll be rewarded five times over.

At that, he took five cockerels and took them up to his lordship. But the lord knew full well that Paul was churning with envy. He didn't want to accept the present, but Paul protested so much that in the end he took it, with the condition that Paul should serve the bird, just as Peter had. All five cocks were cooked, and when they were set on the table, this is what he said to Paul:

Listen, Paul. In my home the custom is for the person who brings the gift to divide it up, and in such a way that all seven of us should get their rightful portion. If you share out well, it will be to your good; if not, you will receive twenty-four strokes of the rod."

Paul thought hard and long, but had not the wit to divide five cockerels among seven people.

When the lord saw that Paul was getting nowhere, he summoned Peter to him.

Peter began to divide the food:

"I find," said Peter, "that your lordship, your ladyship and a cockerel make up a trinity, as do the two young gentlemen and a cock and the two young ladies and a cock as well. I myself and two cockerels are a trinity likewise, and so a good appetite to one and all!"

The entire household burst out laughing at Peter's trickery. Paul was given twenty-four strokes of the rod for his pains, but Peter rewarded with house and land.

He's still alive, if he hasn't died.

The Gallant Cloakmaker

I tell the tale of a cloakmaker, who was poor as a church mouse. But not quite! He had scissors that would not cut, a toothless wife, and then as many children as there are holes in a sieve and then one more. Some days they ate, and other days they didn't, and they only had hominy on Sundays, and not every Sunday at that. But once it happened that a single morsel of gruel was left on the table and enough flies descended upon it that would have eaten the entire pot.

The cloakmaker fell into a rage that even the flies were beggaring him, and slammed his palm down on the table so that twenty of the pests were left dead.

"Well!" thought the cloakmaker, "who would have thought I was so strong? Not me, certainly. Well then, huzzah! Let's go and try our luck!"

Straightaway he carved a board for himself, and on the board wrote in capital letters:

TWENTY AT A GO!

He hung the board around his neck and set out into the wide world. His children wept and implored him to stay at home, and what would they do without him? His wife was no different, but so resolved was he that chains could not have held him. He deeply believed that with his great gallantry he would do well somewhere in the world. And so off he went, on and on, and on his way he came to a great forest. Exhausted, he lay down beside a well. As he lay there, along came the devil with a great buffalo-skin, intending to fill it with water. He caught sight of the cloakmaker and the board with the inscription around his neck.

"Hmm," he thought to himself, "this must be a strong man indeed! He'd make me a good servant."

Straightway he greeted him, and with deep respect:

"Good day to you, earth-dweller!"

"Good day to you," replied the cloakmaker, shortly.

"Are you really so strong that you can smite "twenty at a go"? Heh?"

"Mhhm!" muttered the cloakmaker.

"Will you sign yourself to me as a servant?"

"That I will, if the wages are good!"

They made a quick agreement. The cloakmaker would serve the devil for three years and bring him wood and water. He had no other duties, and when his time was up he would receive a sack of gold.

The gallant cloakmaker clapped his hands together. He said, "Here's my hand on it and no pig's trotter, brother devil. Let him be a dog who breaks his word."

With that they set off for the devil's home, who happened to have exactly as many children as the cloakmaker, or maybe one or two more. As soon as they arrived home the little devils drank up all the water and thrust the buffalo-skin into the cloakmaker's arms to bring more water from the well.

Poor man! He cudgelled his brains to find a solution. He could just about carry the empty buffalo-skin to the well, but full of water he couldn't even tip it! As he pondered the devils tired of waiting and sent one of their number after him. The poor cloakmaker was startled and wondered what would become of him. In his great fear he began digging around the well with a piece of wood.

When the devil arrived, he asked him, "What are you doing, gallant cloakmaker?"

"I thought to myself," replied the cloakmaker, "why should I carry water every day when I can take the whole well with me?"

"Oh, don't do that!" screeched the devil. "My mother's blind and might fall in. I'd rather carry the water in your place!"

"Oh, very well," said the cloakmaker, and they agreed with a good will that the devil would take the water home.

The next day they sent the cloakmaker off for wood, but he should have brought back three cords[2]. When three bundles was quite sufficient for him to carry! He racked his brains over what he could do. But in vain: for all that he was none the wiser. To kill time he began to bundle up the cut-down branches lying in the forest, tying them one by one. The little devils couldn't stand the wait and again sent one of their number after him. The devil arrived just as the cloakmaker was bundling up some wood.

"Hey, what are you up to?" asked the devil.

"What indeed? Don't think I'm going into your forest every day! I'll take the whole lot back at once."

He said this with such rage that the poor devil jumped with fright. It screamed for him not to do so for God's sake, because if he took all the wood that there was home it'd all be burnt and none would remain for the winter. Instead, he'd rather take it home himself a little at a time.

"Well then, you carry it, the devil take you," muttered the gallant cloakmaker.

---

[2] Approximately 3·5 cubic metres.

Meanwhile the devil gripped a great beech by its tip and yanked it down as if to tie it by the roots. As he pulled he cried out, "Quick, come here you gallant cloakmaker and grab this branch! My belt on my britches has broken!"

Well, the cloakmaker could not refuse to come to his aid. He held the tree by the tip, but the moment the devil let go it lashed back and catapulted the cloakmaker over to the opposite edge of the forest, next to a bush. Out of the bush leapt a rabbit and ran off, the cloakmaker in hot pursuit, and as luck would have it in the direction of the devil. The gallant cloakmaker pretended to be very angry and ranted both at the rabbit and the bush.

"Wretched creature! I've leapt across the entire forest for it and I still can't catch it! Just look!"

There was neither end nor breadth to his grumbling!

At home the devils whispered and grumbled amongst themselves and decided that they would put the cloakmaker to one more test, and that if he got the better of them again they would give him his entire wage and send him back where he came from. The next day they sent him off to the fields with the strongest devil to put his strength to the test. The devil took a whip and a club with him. When they arrived at the field, the devil said, "Now, you gallant cloakmaker, show me just how strong you are. Let's see if you can crack this whip as loud as I can!"

"Better that you don't even put it in my hand," replied the cloakmaker, "because I'll crack it so loud your eyes will turn inside out!"

"That's as may be," taunted the devil.

"Well then, you go first," encouraged the cloakmaker.

At that, the devil took the whip and cracked it so loud that the cloakmaker fell on his face with fear.

He could hardly raise himself up, but what he said was, "Well, my fine devilish friend, that wasn't much of a crack, was it? But now cover your eyes unless you want them to turn inside out!"

The devil thought that this was getting beyond a joke and covered his eyes. A devil is nothing without his eyes. This was all the gallant cloakmaker needed: in a flash he took up the club and dealt the devil such a blow that it took ten bathtubs of water to bring him round again.

"Now," said the cloakmaker, once he had with difficulty stood the devil upon his feet, "who's the better whip-cracker, eh?"

"You, you!" whimpered the devil bitterly. "Now let's just go home."

And now fear truly began to spread through the devil's family when they heard of the gallant cloakmaker's freshest exploit. They lost no time filling a sack with gold, gave it to him and told him to go home just so as to see the back of him.

"That I will not!" spluttered the gallant cloakmaker. "If you want me to go home you must take my wage home as well, or I'll stay until my three-year service is up."

They were more frightened of this than of church incense. Rather, they took home the sack of gold just so he wouldn't stay.

The gallant cloakmaker went before, and arrived home earlier than the devil who was carrying his gold. At once he sent his wife into the barn to fill a sack with husks, and told her to come out just as the devil arrived. Then she was to throw the sack up into the hayloft and say, "Look, dear husband, here's a sack full of pure gold. I placed myself in service while you were away."

The wife did as her husband bade her. When the devil saw that even the man's wife was so strong that she could lift a bag of gold up into the hayloft, he thrust his own up as well in his dismay and then raced off as though his life depended upon it. He didn't even dare look back until he had reached the forest.

Here he met a wolf, who asked him, "Where are you running so spiritedly, brother devil?"

"Oh, oh, don't even ask, brother wolf. Have you not heard news of the gallant cloakmaker?"

Then he described to the wolf all the gallant exploits of the man.

The wolf laughed until he cried and the woods resounded. When he finally recovered, he encouraged the devil to go back with him to the cloakmaker and take back the gold from him, for he was a weak, cowardly man.

The devil was inclined to believe him, not so much for what the wolf had said as because he wanted to get back his sack of gold. But he would only go back if they made a yoke and placed both of them in it, because he was afraid that the wolf would desert him at the critical moment.

The wolf didn't mind humouring the devil. They made a yoke, set themselves in it and in this manner entered the cloakmaker's yard, where the cloakmaker's sons happened to be playing. When they saw that the devil was coming with the wolf in a yoke, they believed that he had brought the wolf for them as well.

One called out, "Look, my dad served a wolf as well!"

Another yelled, "Let's keep the devil too! Let's keep the devil too!"

At this the devil was horribly afraid and – hey ho! – ran off complete with yoke and wolf. The wolf tried his best to stop him:

"Don't run, you fool of a devil! Don't be afraid, you ass of a devil!"

But the devil heard nothing and ran as fast as he might. He ran until the wolf's head got caught in the fork of a tree and the yoke broke, and then he ran on. Maybe he is running still.

In this way the gallant cloakmaker freed himself of both devil and wolf, and to this day he and all his kindred live happily from the limitless gold.

Twist in the Tale

Once upon a time in a place there never was and behind the beyond, over the glassy mountains where the corkscrew tailed piglet digs, there lived a poor man. One day the old man went out to plough with his son, and they had hardly turned at the end of the first furrow when the son cried out,

"Look, dad, I've found a key!"

"Ah, that's what it be, a key," said the poor man. "And wouldn't it be just fine if we found a chest to it?"

That was that. The two of them continued ploughing, one, two, three furrows. Then the son cried out for a second time.

"Da-ad, look, I've found the chest as well!"

"They tried the key in the lock, and would you believe it, it fitted perfectly! Then they turned the key and opened in the lid, and what should be inside but a wee mouse with a corkscrew tail.

And if that tail had been longer, so would my tale have been.

Thimble, Comb and Forget It!

Once upon a time and a long time ago, seven times seven lands away and over the glass mountains where the corkscrew-tail piglet digs, there lived a poor man. And this poor man had three sons. The eldest was called Thimble, the middle one Comb and the youngest Forget It.

One day the poor man said to Thimble, "Off with you, son, go and see the world and learn something."

Off went Thimble. He was away for a whole year, visiting the countries of the world and seeing many things and not seeing other things, none of which I'll tell to you. It's enough to say that one year later he returned to his father. On Thimble's arrival, the old man said to the middle son, "Now, Comb, my dear boy, now it's your turn to see the world and keep up with your older brother."

And off went Comb, all over the world. Wherever he went he saw many things, but of what he saw or didn't see I'll tell you nothing. It's enough to say that a year later he returned, and then the youngest son, whose name was…what was it….oh dear, I don't remember…

(And somebody calls out, "Forget it!")

"Oh all right, I will…"

THE END